NICKELODEON

The BACKYARDIGANS™

The Trash Planet

adapted by Emily Sollinger

based on the screenplay "Garbage Trek" by Robert Scull

illustrated by The Artifact Group

Ready-to-Read

SIMON SPOTLIGHT/NICKELODEON
New York   London   Toronto   Sydney

Based on the TV series *Nick Jr. The Backyardigans*™ as seen on Nick Jr.®

SIMON SPOTLIGHT
An imprint of Simon & Schuster Children's Publishing Division
1230 Avenue of the Americas, New York, New York 10020
© 2009 Viacom International Inc. All rights reserved.
NICK JR., *Nick Jr. The Backyardigans*, and all related titles, logos, and characters are trademarks
of Viacom International Inc. NELVANA™ Nelvana Limited. CORUS™ Corus Entertainment Inc.
All rights reserved, including the right of reproduction in whole or in part in any form.
SIMON SPOTLIGHT, READY-TO-READ, and colophon are registered trademarks
of Simon & Schuster, Inc.
Manufactured in the United States of America
First Edition
2 4 6 8 10 9 7 5 3 1
Library of Congress Cataloging-in-Publication Data
Sollinger, Emily.
The trash planet /adapted by Emily Sollinger. —1st ed.
p. cm. — (Ready-to-read)
"Nick Jr. The backyardigans."
"Adapted from the episode: Garbage trek, by Robert Scull."
ISBN-13: 978-1-4169-6868-9
ISBN-10: 1-4169-6868-7
I. Backyardigans (Television program) II. Title.
PZ7.S6953Tr 2009
2008002651

I am  Captain .
TRASH TASHA

I collect  in
TRASH

outer space.

I am  Grabber .
TRASH AUSTIN

I am Grabber .
TRASH UNIQUA

We find 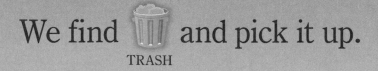 and pick it up.

TRASH

We ride through outer space

in a big .

SPACESHIP

"Alert! Alert!" calls

 Grabber .

TRASH   AUSTIN

The lights flash.

"  **PLANET** Trashica is ready for pickup," **AUSTIN** tells his team.

" **TRASH** , here we come!"

The grabbers
TRASH

move from  to  .
PLANET   PLANET

They fill their  with lots

of .

TRUCK

TRASH

Beep beep!

"Someone is calling for help,"

says Grabber .

TRASH   AUSTIN

"We have to find them," says

 Captain .

TRASH   TASHA

They beam down to the .

PLANET

and her team

TASHA

follow the call.

It is Alien

TYRONE

and Alien

PABLO

.

They take the

TRASH

from

TASHA

's

SPACESHIP

.

They put it in their own  SPACESHIP .

They are not really in trouble.

"They tricked us!" shouts

TRASH Captain TASHA .

But it is too late.

Alien TYRONE and Alien PABLO

speed away on their SPACESHIP .

"We love  !" they say.

TRASH

"All of our  is gone!" cries .

TRASH

TASHA

"We need to find more!" says .

UNIQUA

"Look! There is a

PLANET

filled with !" says .

TRASH

AUSTIN

"But we have to watch out

for that big black ⬤."

HOLE

Beep beep!

It is another call for help.

"The aliens want to trick us

again," says .
TASHA

"The sound is inside the black 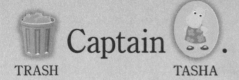,"
HOLE

says Grabber 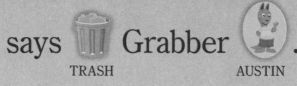.
TRASH AUSTIN

"Someone really is stuck."

"We will help them!" says

 Captain .
TRASH TASHA

"We need  !" calls Alien PABLO.

"Our SPACESHIP runs

on TRASH power."

"And we have too much ," says Grabber .

TRASH   TRASH   UNIQUA

"Our is too heavy."

SPACESHIP

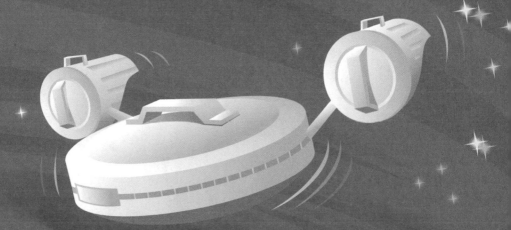

TASHA pushes a button.

The TRASH flies out.

The alien SPACESHIP eats the TRASH.

"You saved us!" say PABLO and  TYRONE.

The alien
SPACESHIP

pulls Captain 's
TRASH   TASHA   SPACESHIP

out of the big black .
HOLE

"You saved us!" says .
TASHA

"That was a great adventure!"

TRASH

says .

TYRONE

"Who wants a snack?" asks .

TASHA